Explosive Passion

SEALed for You

Marissa Dobson

Published by Dobson Ink
Printed in the United States of America
ISBN: 978-1-939978-91-2

Dedication

To all the men and woman in the military who serve our country, and their families.

Contents

Navy SEAL Jared "Boom" Taylor is supposed to chaperone his best friend's sister home, but with a car malfunction and an impending storm, the plan goes out the window. Finding shelter in an abandoned cabin, with the one woman he can't get off his mind, is his chance to prove to her that military men are worth the added effort.

Boutique owner Wynn Diamond is on the verge of some exciting opportunities and with each new door opening things become more unnerving. Deciding to take refuge in a one-night stand to let off some steam, she never thought it would turn into more.

Could a one-night stand with a man in uniform actually be the forever she had been looking for?

Chapter One

"Don't you dare!" Jared "Boom" Taylor slammed his hand on the steering wheel as the rental car sputtered to a stop on the side of the country road. This couldn't be happening. He had promised to get Wynn back to Virginia Beach. With the coughing and wheezing of the car, they weren't going anywhere.

"Boom?" Wynn Diamond, his best friend's baby sister, turned in the passenger seat to look at him. "What have you done?"

His lips curled up at the corner and he chuckled. "Why do women always assume the man did something when things go wrong?"

"You were driving."

He glanced down at the dashboard, rooting around for a hidden switch, anything that would reverse what she was claiming he did. His fingers ran over the smooth dashboard; he pushed against it looking for a hidden door with a switch. Yet he found nothing.

"What are you doing?" She raised an eyebrow at him, completely puzzled.

"Looking for this magical switch that you imply makes a car act like this." With a smirk, he glanced over at her. "I've been driving for years and I've never known there was one. Would you like to show me where it is?"

"Boom…"

"Or maybe you're saying before we left Ace and Gwen's wedding reception I tampered under the hood so that this would happen."

"With the farewell you put into action, no one would have missed you breaking the car," she teased.

When Ace asked Boom to be the best man, he gave him the stipulation that he wasn't to blow up anything during his wedding duties. As SEAL Team Two's demolitions expert, it wasn't possible for him not to do something that would create a loud boom to send the newlyweds off. It left him with only one course of action; he hired someone to do it for him. Lighting the evening sky with pink and white hearts was his way of giving the newlyweds a romantic farewell and keeping with his usual performance.

"I have to admit, it was some send off." Her comment pulled him back from remembering his amazing farewell.

"As best man, it was my duty to send them off in style." He glanced over at Wynn in her pale blue bridesmaid's dress—he was sure the color had a special name that only a woman would be able to tell him—her blonde shoulder-length hair pulled up, leaving only ringlets hanging down.

"At least you didn't blow up the place." She smirked at her smartass comment.

He had blown up plenty of buildings in the past, but that wasn't a trip down memory lane he wanted to take. Placing his hand on the door handle, he peeled his gaze from her. "I'll see if I can fix this." He had to do something to get the car started again or she was going to freeze in that strapless dress as the temperatures plummeted.

He slipped out of the car, quickly closing the door behind him, and tugged his tuxedo jacket closed. The air had turned cold, announcing the storm that would soon be blanketing the area. It was rare for this part of Virginia to be hit with such a strong hurricane, but they had one barreling toward them that promised to be disastrous. If he didn't get the car going soon, they'd have to find a place to bunker down. As the wind picked up he spotted a small cabin through the trees, maybe it would have a phone, because his cell phone had no reception.

Every SEAL had to have basic mechanical skills, but propping open the hood he didn't have hope that it was something he could fix. What he needed was Bad Billy—a fellow SEAL—who could fix anything with an engine, but the rest of the team had stayed behind. They wanted to have a night to celebrate that the oldest of the team, besides Lieutenant Commander Mac García, had married.

Knowing the rest of the team was off partying while he had agreed to see Wynn home sent a twinge of jealousy though him. Being the man he was, Boom couldn't see Wynn traveling alone. When the youngest Diamond sibling, Lucky, announced he had to leave the wedding reception early for military duty; it left Boom to step up and escort her home.

Pushing the thought from his mind, he leaned under the hood and grabbed the dipstick to check the oil level. Nothing. There was just nothing on the dipstick. "You've got to be shitting me!"

The passenger door opened. "What is it?"

"We're not going anywhere." He waved the dipstick at her. "There's not a drop of oil in the bloody thing. Everything's seized up because of it."

"What are we going to do?"

"Find a phone." He tipped his head in the direction he'd seen the cabin. "I'm going to see if I can find one there."

She glanced where he nodded. "I don't see anything."

"There's a cabin about a hundred feet from the road. Maybe there's a phone. I can call the rental car company and they can bring us a new car."

"It's nearly midnight. No one's going to bring us a new one now."

"Well, hopefully we can at least find somewhere warm, 'cause we'll freeze in the car." He moved around to the back of the car and opened the trunk.

"What are you doing?"

"If we're going to be stuck here tonight, I don't want to have to come back for your bag." He slipped it over his shoulder, before grabbing the jeans and sweater he wore earlier and a small box. "Why do women always pack so much?" he joked, pretending to do curls with the weight.

"Considering I came up two days before the wedding, I barely packed anything." She reached for the bag but he held it out of the way. "I'll take it if it's too heavy for the big SEAL."

Rolling his eyes, he slammed the trunk and headed for the trees. "Whatever you say."

"We can't go banging on someone's door at this time of night."

He paused just outside the line of trees. "Do you want to stay in the car and freeze?"

"No, but this dress and shoes aren't for walking through the woods." She pulled up the hem of her skirt and carefully stepped toward him.

"I could carry you."

"Thank you, but I'll pass on that." She stepped off the pavement and her heels sank a little into the ground beneath her feet. "You planned this, didn't you? You wanted me all to yourself and devised this car malfunction to do it," she teased. It was true they had spent much of the last few weeks together but even he wasn't as deceiving as that.

"Give me a little credit." His lips curled into a smile. "For a beautiful woman like you, I would have planned it somewhere better than an abandoned cabin. We'd have broken down in front of a five-star resort or a beautiful cabin with amazing views. Something special that you'd never forget."

She paused, looking at him. Had he done something like that in the past? She shook her head, pushing the idea away. He was gorgeous and didn't need to do anything like that to get a woman into bed with him. She had no doubt that if he wanted them, they'd be lined up around the block waiting their turn. A twinge of jealousy coursed through her. She didn't want to think of other women in his bed. Instead, she glanced up at the cabin. "What if no one is there?"

"I don't think anyone's there. It looks abandoned." He slipped his arm lightly around her waist, making sure she was steady.

"We'll break in then?"

"They'll understand. We're miles from anywhere, nothing is in walking distance, and there won't be cars passing at this time of night. We have no other choice." He led her through the trees, bringing the cabin into view. It was a small one-story building, which looked to be well cared-for but empty for some time, like a vacation spot. *This is an odd place for a vacation home, but to each their own.*

As they crossed the empty space between road and cabin, the first raindrops began to fall. "Just what we need," he bitched.

"I love a good storm. We don't get nearly enough."

"Storms are fine, it's more the fact we need suitable shelter and heat before things pick up too badly." He was used to harsh conditions and could survive a night in the cold, but Wynn was another story. Ace would kill him if something happened to her. "Come along, let's get inside."

Chapter Two

The fire crackled, sending sparks up the chimney and heat through the room. Wynn stood in front of it with her hands outstretched, trying to chase the chill from her bones. The short walk from the car had frozen her to the bone. She had changed into her jeans but the only sweater she'd brought with her did very little to ease her discomfort.

For a day that had been so perfect, this was a dramatic change. Going from a picture-perfect wedding to this abandoned cabin with a man she knew all her life, and lusted after. Before Ace and Gwen began planning their wedding, Wynn had only seen Boom a handful of times since he joined the military. He was Ace's best friend making him an important part in the wedding planning, and the time together had brought all those feeling rushing back. If he wasn't her brother's best friend and a SEAL, she might want to get to know him better. Naked better, that was.

The little tease of his hand around her waist as they made their way from the car only heated the fire within her. She wanted more of his gentle touch, to feel his hands on the most intimate parts of her body.

She shook her head, trying to push the thoughts away. She couldn't afford to think like that, especially not alone with him in a tiny cabin. It was too romantic with the glow of the fire and the wind and rain beating against the walls.

Boom came to stand next to her in front of the fire. "Here, this should warm you." He offered her a steaming cup of coffee.

"Where did you get this?"

"The box of stuff I carried from the car." He took a sip from his own mug. "It was a few left over things from the wedding that your mom asked me to bring back. Coffee, a container of berries, some cookies, and left over favors."

"Great, we have coffee and cookies to survive on."

"We're not going to be here long enough to worry about needing food to survive." He sat the coffee on the mantel.

"How do you figure? There's no phone here, the car is dead; with this storm, how are we going to get out of here?" Desperation pitched her voice higher.

"Shhh…" He touched her shoulder. When she didn't move away, he pulled her into a hug. "I'll get us out of here. First light I'll set out for a phone."

"It could be miles away."

"I've gone longer in training. I'll make it wherever the phone is. We've just got to wait until morning. We're safe and warm here." His hand ran along her shoulder, drawing small circles against the fabric of her sweater. "I'll get you out of this mess and everything will be fine."

Her blood ran hot from his touch, and unless she was going to give in to temptation she needed to cool her thoughts. She forced her gaze out the window and focused on the impending storm, instead of the man before her. Part of her wanted to press herself tighter against his ever-so-toned body, only to stop as thoughts of his career pushed their way into her mind.

Having her brother risk life and limb as a SEAL was enough; she sure didn't want her man doing it. She couldn't understand how Gwen was willing to stand by and have Ace risk everything, especially now that there was a child on its way. Her brother would be a father in less than two months. She thought maybe he'd leave the SEALs when his commitment was up and finally get a safe job, only to find out he had no intention of leaving his assignment and would re-up at the end of the year. What kind of life was that for Gwen and the baby? She shook her head. It wasn't a life she'd want. She wanted a man that would be there by her side.

He turned toward her, taking the coffee from her, setting it aside. She stood there, not sure what to do as his hand slid down her arm. His very touch was mesmerizing, keeping her locked in a trance watching him. It was that electricity that wouldn't let her go even if she wanted it to.

"I'm going to kiss you." Without giving her a moment to hesitate, he leaned into her and claimed her lips with his own. The spiciness from the coffee lingered on his lips, mixing with her vanilla lip-gloss. He used his tongue to gently ease her mouth open, giving him entrance and allowing their tongues to dance together. She leaned closer, her hand traveling up his chest; he kissed her one final time before pulling back.

When she finally regained herself, she stepped out of his embrace. "We shouldn't have done that."

"Why not?"

"Which reason should I give you, because I have a few?" When he didn't answer, she continued. "You're a SEAL, and I never get involved with military men. Not to mention Ace would have a fit; you're his best friend."

"Shouldn't that be a good thing? Then he'd know his baby sister was in good hands."

"I don't get involved with military men," she repeated, more determined than before. Only this time, she wasn't sure if she was trying to convince him or herself.

"Make an exception, and it won't be something you regret." He advanced toward her, closing the distance she had put between them only seconds before. "We're here together for a reason."

"Yeah, because the car broke down," she reminded him.

"I've always believed things happen for a reason." He laid a hand on her forearm. "Rental cars go through inspections every time they come in. I didn't see a leak when I pulled it from the hotel parking lot. For it to have seized up the engine as it did means there's no oil left in the whole damn thing, yet it made it to the hotel just fine yesterday."

"Are you saying someone did this to get us stranded together? They could have gotten us killed."

He shook his head. "Not someone, but maybe a something. A master plan, a God, whatever you believe."

"After everything you've seen, how can you believe there's something beyond what we can see with the naked eye?"

"How can I not? I've been in positions I never thought I'd make it out of, yet somehow I did. I believe there's been something that has kept me and the rest of the team safe. Otherwise I wouldn't still be here."

Unable to fathom that he believed in a higher being, she took a step back and perched herself on the armrest of the sofa. "You're the team's demolitions expert; I've heard stories of things blowing up all around you, including IED's, and still you come away untouched."

"That's why I believe." He shoved his hands into the pockets of his jeans. "I've seen so many lose a body part or worse, their lives, because of IED's, yet I've survived. There has to be a reason that I'm still here; some great purpose."

"Right there is the reason I don't get involved with military men." He stared at her as if he didn't understand. "There's too much risk involved with your job. It's bad enough worrying about Ace and Lucky every time they're deployed. I don't need another man in my life to worry about."

"So you'd rather play it safe and not love?" He raised an eyebrow.

"Safe isn't a bad thing, and as for love I'm open to it for someone with a safe job. You're not safe." She dragged her hand through her hair-sprayed, thick hair, tugging the blonde locks away from her face.

"Fine, not long-term. What about tonight?"

"Tonight." The word came out on a whisper. In that moment to have even just one night with him sounded like paradise. It would be the first time she lived on the edge instead of just playing things by the book. Designing the specialty stuff she carried in her little boutique just off the boardwalk took all her time. There was nothing left over for a relationship, leaving her lonely.

Giving into the flirtation that had been playing them for weeks, she nodded. "Tonight…only."

 Chapter Three

Boom couldn't keep the smirk off his face. Since he began spending time with her during the wedding planning, he couldn't keep his thoughts off her. The little girl from his childhood had been replaced by a woman that had her life together. She was making everything she always wanted happen and she never seemed happier. Her smile lit up the room, and the way her gaze traveled over him, as if she was thinking of him naked, made him want to show her what he had to offer. This one night he was going to make it turn into much more. It might be his only shot with her and he wasn't going to let it slip past. If he was going to convince her that this could work, he was going to have a fight on his hands; one that might be the toughest he'd ever experienced in all his years in the military. Though he had a feeling Wynn Diamond was a woman worth fighting for.

"I've found blankets in the closet; I'll make us a bed in front of the fire and we'll open the bottle of wine I brought." He winked at her before strolling toward where he found the blankets.

"I'll get the wine."

"It's on the counter." He tipped his head to the other side of the cabin, where a bar divided the kitchen and living room. While she went for the wine he went down the short hallway that led to the only bedroom and bathroom.

Minutes later, he had a makeshift bed spread out before the fire. With no heat besides what came from the fireplace, they had no other option but to make a bed on the floor if they wanted to stay warm. With all the blankets he could find, and pillows from the bed spread out he turned back to her.

"Last chance to change your mind." There would be no going back from this. She was going to be his.

"I want you…even if it's only for one night." She handed him the glass of wine before taking a sip out of her own glass.

Not wanting to spoil the mood, he took a sip of his wine before setting it aside and keeping quiet. There was no reason to argue about the one night comment now. "Come, gorgeous." He pulled her toward the fireplace.

They eased down onto the blankets and he pressed his lips to hers softly. Letting each new kiss explore a little deeper, until the passion between them ignited like the fire they sat in front of. Their tongues danced together, giving him the taste of the wine on her lips, and the air sizzled around them. There was enough heat between them to warm the place without the fire.

Their time together in this special place was short and he didn't want to miss a second of it. He broke their kiss to lift her sweater over her head. "You have too many clothes on."

"You too." She grabbed the waist of his sweater and pulled it off.

"Lay back." As she did what he asked, he let his hands slide down her curves until he unbuttoned her jeans and pulled them slowly down her legs. The sexy pale blue panties that matched her bra called to him, he grabbed them with his teeth and pulled them away. Laying her bare sent desire racing through him. No longer able to control himself, he slid the panties off the rest of the way before easing her legs open.

She leaned forward, dragging her hand over his head, fingers sliding over his buzz cut. He pushed her back gently, making her lay flat once again, and pressed his lips to her stomach. He kissed around her bellybutton, grazing his teeth along her tender flesh. He stroked her thighs with his fingertips, until with every touch she arched into him, demanding more. Nudging her legs further apart, his fingers delved inside her and she met the teasing thrusts eagerly. A demanding moan vibrated through her body. Passion drove his hand harder and faster.

The trail of wicked kisses tingled over the insides of her thighs. He slipped his fingers from her, quickly replacing them with his mouth, while his hands moved to her hips, holding her against him as she wiggled in desire. Tiny nips and gentle licks flicked over her sweet spot, nearly driving her over the edge. "Boom!" Her fingernails dug into his shoulders until he could feel the skin break and blood trickle from the tiny moon shapes.

"I want you...please, Jared!" The way she called out his given name made it more intimate. It had been a very long time since someone called him anything but Boom.

He slid up her body until he hovered over her. With one hand, he unhooked the front clasp of her black lace bra, baring her completely to him. "Damn, you're beautiful!" He trailed wet, teasing kisses to each of her hard dusky pink nipples. Drawing one into his mouth, he let his tongue circle around it, before grazing his teeth along it and letting it slip from his mouth, moving to the other one.

"Please…" That one simple word, deeply laced with desire, sped his pace.

"Anything for you, Wynn." He pulled away long enough to shed the rest of his clothes. Her gaze scorched as it swept over him. "Do you like what you see, beautiful?"

"Maybe," she said coyly.

"Humm, just maybe? Let's see what we can do about that." Confidence and cockiness surged through him. He lowered himself, careful to stay just above her.

"Please, I want you now."

"What's the rush? We have all night."

"Then give it to me now, and we can have another round or two later." There was a twinkle in her eye.

"Mmm, a woman after my own heart." He placed his hands gently on her thighs, spreading them further, giving him the access he desired. He teased her sensitive flesh with his fingers before finally sliding himself into her warm wet core until he filled her completely. A cry of desire and need escaped her lips. Her body arched and she nibbled the side of his neck.

Her moans of pleasure spurred him faster. His hips increased pace, driving forcefully into her with each thrust. Their bodies, bound together, found a rhythm; passion shot through him, made him desperate for release. He fought the ecstasy, fought to hang on and drive her to climax. Digging her nails into his back, she writhed. Their lips met again and again. She screamed against his mouth and he held on for another few seconds, prolonging the beautiful agony until finally reaching release.

He knew he wanted more of her, doubted he would ever get enough. He collapsed next to her, their legs entwined, his energy spent for the moment. She curled her body into his, her hand resting on his chest.

"Looks as though you enjoyed that." He wrapped his arms around her.

"Oh yes." She lazily ran a hand up and down his chest. "Ready for another round?"

He snickered. "I'm a SEAL; I'm always ready."

Chapter Four

The fire cast a faint glow over the room as it began to die down, as the fire died so did their need, leaving behind exhaustion. Wynn lay cuddled against Boom's body, her hand lying across his chest, holding him close while her mind screamed for her to run. Giving in to desire for one night with him was supposed to relieve her longing for him. Instead, it already wasn't enough. She wanted more.

No! One night, that's it. She wouldn't put herself through what she witnessed so many military spouses suffer through. It was no life worrying that he wouldn't come home, or waiting by the phone for him to call, or at the computer for an email. That wasn't something she could do. She needed a man who would be there with her, by her side, not off fighting against the things that go bump in the night.

She had done one-night stands in the past and each time it released sexual tension, rejuvenated her, and allowed her to put sex on the back burner for a while. With Boom, it did the complete opposite: she wanted more of him in every way.

"What's on your mind?" His fingers rubbed down her arm.

"This isn't how it's supposed to work."

"What isn't?"

"This." She forced herself to stop tracing the lines of his abs and leaned up on her elbow. "One-night stands; it's about sex and then both people go about their lives. They don't lay here and cuddle."

"What would you prefer? We each go to our own place in the cabin? Maybe I sleep in the kitchen?" He smirked. "But if I may say something without making you angry…you were the one cuddling with me."

"What?" Surprised, she raised an eyebrow at him, but realized he was right and went to pull away.

"Not that I'm complaining, but your naked body was pressed against mine." He closed the distance she had put between them. "You're the one that said tonight only, not me."

Pressing her back against the corner of the sofa, the wood digging into her skin, she tried to ground herself. "You agreed."

"Only that I'd have you tonight."

"You conceited, bastard!" She tried to pull the blanket from him so she could get up without baring her nakedness to him.

"I asked you before to let me show you what I could give you. Tonight was the first part and I'm not giving up now. What are you so afraid of?"

She let her head fall back against the cushion, trying to figure out the best way to answer his question. She wanted to tell him she wasn't afraid, but that wasn't the case, she was terrified she'd give him her heart and he wouldn't come back.

"Living here, surrounded by so many military families, dealing with Ace and Lucky's careers, I'm all too aware of the dangers."

"Ace and I were made for this, it's what we've wanted all our lives. Nothing's going to happen to us."

"Bullshit." She squared her shoulders, refusing to let her emotions control her. "One of the missions could be the last, leaving me heartbroken and alone. I can't do that."

"Yet, yesterday you stood by while your best friend did that very thing, and you gave her your blessing."

"Ace is a stubborn man. He'll come back to her. He wouldn't let some terrorist stand between him and Gwen, not now when they just found each other again." Jealousy teased through her with the knowledge that Gwen and Ace had something that she wanted, but was denying herself. *No, Boom isn't the right one. Someday the right man will come and I'll have it too.*

"As would I." He placed his hand over hers. "We do this job to protect America, to keep you safe, to allow our children to be born into a world where they don't have to fear what might happen. We want to make this country safe so that we don't have a repeat of nine-eleven or any of the other disasters that have happened. Don't you want your niece to be brought into a world where she can live free and safe?"

"I get why you do it and I admire it. Ace, Lucky, you, and the rest are my heroes. You risk yourself so that others can enjoy life without truly understanding the dangers that surround us." She reached out and cupped his cheek. "I just don't want my heart broken."

He tipped his head into her hand and kissed her palm. "Sweet cheeks, I'm not going to break your heart."

Everything in her wanted to believe his words. She wanted to believe that he'd always come back to her, no matter what he faced, but it scared the hell out of her.

"Wynn, I've never wanted a woman the way I want you—like a lit match in a powder magazine. Give us a chance."

"I can't." She tugged the blanket tight against her. "I need a man who will be there; one I can snuggle against each night. Being with a military man is like being single half the time."

"But the other half is like being newlyweds. It makes up for any time away."

"It's not like you're normal military, where you deploy for six months to a year. Your deployment rotation is faster; even when you're not deployed, you're still not actually home. Most of your training isn't done here." She glanced toward the fire. "You're just gone too much."

"That's not something I can change, but the time we're together will be unbelievable." He ran the back of his finger along her jawline. "Wouldn't that make up for what time I'm gone?"

"Please, Jared…you're an amazing man, but I just can't." She shook her head over and over, as if it would solidify the decision in her heart.

"I'm not going to stop fighting for you."

Unable to handle it any longer she slipped past him, grabbed her clothes, and headed to the bathroom. She needed to get away from him before he wore down her resistance further. Tears sprang to her eyes, and she fought to keep them from falling. *I can't do this…not with him.*

Chapter Five

After getting dressed, Wynn snuck out the back of the house. With nowhere else to go, she stood on the small porch at the back of the cabin, trying to gather herself. The sex had been amazing, better than she could have hoped for, and that's what made it so much harder. She wanted what Gwen had. She'd longed for and searched for it, but had never found it.

In the past few weeks she got to know a different side of Boom, one that hadn't been there when they were children. He was a good man, one that she had started to fall hard for. Now one amazing evening of sex and she couldn't get enough of him. He could give her everything she wanted, except himself; that, she'd only get part-time. The military would always have the other half. All these years she said she wouldn't make that sacrifice. She already did when it came to her brothers, she wouldn't do it with her husband. Now for the first time she wondered if her rule was standing in the way of her happiness.

Could a relationship with Boom really work, even with him gone so often? Or would resentment at being left alone eventually set in? Between designing the latest fashions for her boutique and running the shop, she was busy. She needed a man who would understand her creative whims and wouldn't fuss if she spent all night in her studio or slipped out of bed in the middle of the night because an idea came to her that she had to get down on paper.

The future could get even more hectic with the latest offer she received. Just three days before the wedding she got the offer of a lifetime. Not wanting to steal the spotlight from Ace and Gwen, she kept it to herself. Plus, it was best to wait until the ink dried on the contract before official announcements were shared. Then they could really celebrate, before the real work set in.

She shook her head as the realization of what she wanted sank in. It wasn't fair that she expected her man to accept her career when she couldn't accept his. If he was military and she cared for him, then she should accept it. How could she expect someone to do it for her if she wasn't willing to do it for them? Relationships were give and take, if she wanted to explore where things could go with Boom she'd have to accept his choice of careers.

"It's too cold for you to be out here without something warmer on." He wrapped a blanket around her shoulders.

She took hold of the blanket so it wouldn't fall onto the wet porch and turned to face him. "I didn't hear you come out."

"I came around the front, because I checked the car first. When I didn't find you in the bathroom I thought you'd taken refuge in the car out of the howling wind."

"I didn't even think about it." The wind picked up and her body shivered against the assault. "I just needed a few minutes to get my thoughts together."

"I figured. You've been out here twenty minutes. It's time to come in before you catch your death. If you want me to stay in the car, I will."

"What makes you think I can't handle the cold but you can?" Her sadness turned to anger, and it showed in her voice.

"It's cold but not the worst weather I've had to deal with by far. I'd survive." He held up his hand, stopping her as she started to say something. "This has nothing to do with you being a woman, so don't pull that card with me. You've never had to deal with the shit I have, my body is used to it. I barely feel the cold any longer. Now, please come inside."

With one last glance up at the darkening sky, she nodded. "I wouldn't make you sleep in the car."

"I never thought you would, but I offered." He laid his hand on the small of her back and led her to the door. "I didn't mean to upset you."

Stepping into the warmth, she realized how cold she was. Her teeth chattered and her hands shook. "Come sit with me by the fire." Too cold to wait to see if he followed, she dashed forward to the warmth of the fireplace.

Without a word, he followed her, keeping a little bit of distance between them. He sat down on the chair furthest from the fire.

Damn did he look fine sitting there like he didn't have a care in the world! The heather gray sweater was pulled tight across his chest, showing off the contours of his abs, and she wanted to run her hands over them again. She forced herself to stay where she was, her gaze on the fireplace away from his perfect body.

"Outside I realized something…" She took a deep breath and forced herself to continue. "I work crazy hours, sometimes all night or for days at a time, only crashing for an hour or two. If I expect someone to accept that, then I should be willing to accept their job. Don't get me wrong, your job is dangerous and I don't like it, but I should at least try."

"What are you saying, Wynn?"

"I don't know what's between us or where it could go but I could try to explore it." She glanced back at him. "I've always wished you weren't a SEAL, then I could allow more than just indulging in flirtation. These past few weeks while we've been helping to plan the wedding for Gwen and Ace I've seen a whole different side to you, one that goes deeper than flirtation; I want the chance to explore it, to see where it could lead."

He leaned forward, his elbows on his knees. "I told you before I'm not going to stop fighting for you. If you take this next step you better be ready for the real thing."

She swallowed the lump that had formed in her throat. "I guess I am."

"I'm not saying it's going to be easy, and some days are going to be an uphill battle. You might even ask yourself why the hell you're doing it. However, I promise you that every chance I get I'm going to prove to you how amazing things can be between us. On the bad days I want you to remember all the good times we have together."

"I'll try." Her heart raced and doubts rushed through her mind. *I must be crazy, breaking my one rule for relationships.*

"Doubting yourself already?" She glanced at him, her eyebrow raised, and he added. "Your body went rigid. It's a clear-cut sign of doubt or fear. In your case, I think both."

"Maybe a little, but didn't you say you'd make it worth it?" she taunted.

"I did." He stretched his long legs out in front of him and rose.

"Where are you going?"

"Wedding snacks. Get comfortable, I'm going to make this a night you won't forget."

The way the words rolled off his tongue made her wonder what he had in mind. With her sweater falling to just past her upper thigh, she slipped out of her damp jeans and back onto the makeshift bed. She'd make tonight count and take tomorrow as it came. Ace's words echoed in her head. *Tomorrow's never guaranteed...*

Chapter Six

Not taking any risks with the one chance he had to eliminate the doubt he saw in Wynn's eyes, he grabbed the open bottle of wine and a plastic container of strawberries and raspberries. Tonight he was going to show her all the positive things he could offer, because without a doubt the negatives would be rearing their ugly heads soon enough. The better he could show her how things would be when he was there, the less she'd doubt what was happening between them. At least that's what the logical part of him said. The rest of him just wanted to get her naked again.

Closing the distance to her, he chuckled. He was falling for a woman that wouldn't be just another fling. Only a short time ago he tried to sway Ace from getting involved with Gwen. The situation might have been different, but still set forth the same results; the only difference was the child that Ace and Gwen were expecting in less than a month. *Oh how the mighty have fallen to the wiles of women.* He smirked and pushed the thoughts aside, his attention falling where it deserved to be: on the amazing Wynn.

"What do you have there?" She smoothed the blanket around her hips.

"Berries and champagne would have been better but wine will have to do in a pinch." He topped off her glass before setting the bottle on the end table. "I'm going to feed you strawberries and we're going to talk."

"Talk?" Surprise laced her voice.

"Yes. Though we've run into each other for years at parties Ace threw, or family events he invited me to, and over the last several weeks planning the wedding, we've never really gotten to know each other. So let's start there, and then, well, I have other plans before the night is over." He took hold of the stem of the first strawberry. "You said before that your business takes a lot of your time, tell me about it."

"Roll of the Diamond, it's a little fashionable boutique just off the boardwalk. We only sell my designs there. It's not huge, but it's what I love doing. We also do custom orders, like Gwen's wedding dress and my bridesmaid dress. The custom orders extend from everything to shirts, pants, a whole wardrobe, or even wedding attire."

"I can see the passion in your eyes when you speak of the boutique. You love your work just as I love mine." He dangled a strawberry in front of her lips, waiting for her to take a bite.

"I know." She leaned just a little forward, lips closing around the strawberry; some of the rich juices drizzled down the corner of her mouth.

Without thinking about it, he ran his finger from her chin up to the corner of her lip to catch the liquid and licked his finger. Their gazes locked while she ate the last half of the berry.

"I know you could never be anything other than what you are. You're a SEAL; it's not just your job, it's you, down to the very core. I know the dedication you have because I've seen it in Ace. You both are two sides of the same coin."

He took a raspberry from the dish and popped it in his mouth. "I hadn't planned to bring my work up tonight."

"But it seeps in." She took the raspberry he offered. "That's what the military does. It affects every aspect of your life, making everything else fold around it in order to survive."

"I'm seeing those doubts again."

"Actually, just the opposite." She took a long sip of the wine. "Unlike Gwen, I didn't grow up with the military, but I have seen how it affects a life because of my brothers. Things can never be planned because deployments or training can come up; holidays and family events are missed for the same reasons. In a way, my life is just as complicated. I don't deploy at a moment's notice as you do, but the boutique demands everything of me. Maybe this type of relationship is one that can suit us both."

"What's that supposed to mean?"

"We're both busy and enjoy our work, but it limits what we have to give to someone else. Taking this as it might be, and cherishing the moments we have together... There's no reason we both can't be devoted to what we love and still have time together. I have a feeling those times would be magical all on their own."

"Oh, my beautiful Wynn, they will be magical, but as I told you before, I'm in this for the long run. I'm not going to be satisfied with brief encounters when our ships pass in the night and I don't think you will be either."

"How do you know what I'd be satisfied with?" She set the wineglass aside and moved up against the pillows. "I've done one-night stands and flings and they work for me. Boyfriends can't understand my work obsession, even ones who are as dedicated to their profession. Too many of them see my designs as a hobby, not a business, but damn it, Roll of the Diamond is more than just a hobby or a way to make a living. It's what I do, and making a living is a lot more than just what my boutique can do."

"Wow, Wynn, I meant no…"

"No, I'm the one that's sorry." She dragged her fingers through her hair. "I love my business, but my mother just thinks it's a hobby. Now that Ace has married and there's a granddaughter on the way, she thinks I should be next. Give up my boutique, settle down and become a baby machine. That's not me."

"I never said it was." He laid his hand on her arm, smoothing up and down it. "Your family always seemed supportive."

"My parents are supportive of Ace and Lucky, but the hidden secret is that they hate my work. My designs are too edgy and revealing; they want me to close up shop and settle down with a nice man who can take care of me. That's not me. I'm not Suzie homemaker who's

42

happy being barefoot and pregnant. I want a life and a career of my own. Why should I have to choose?"

"You shouldn't. You can have everything you want and be married, even have some munchkins if that's what you want."

He hated to see her so frustrated. The very idea that her parents pressured her to give up something she loved ate at his stomach. He had been there with his own parents, and in the end it only made things tense between them. A trip home hadn't happened in years, even phone calls to his parents were effectively nonexistent between them because of the tension over his choice of careers. He didn't like the idea that Wynn was suffering with the same thing. Maybe he'd talk with Ace and they'd see if the two of them could make the Diamond parents lay off Wynn's career choice.

Chapter Seven

Discussing her family and their views on her boutique made Wynn's stomach churn. All her life she'd strived for her parent's approval. The boutique was the first thing that was really against what they wanted for her. It was the one thing she wanted more than anything else was and she wasn't about to give it up.

"Three days ago I received a call from New York. I kept it to myself because I knew what my parents' reaction would be, and I didn't want to spoil the wedding." She paused, unable to refuse when he dangled another strawberry in front of her.

"What did they want?" He pushed as she enjoyed the sweet berry.

"Me…well, my designs." She swallowed, pushing the anxiety down. "I have ten days to prepare ten designs for them to evaluate. If they like them, I'll have a small section in a boutique on Fifth Avenue in New York City."

"That's wonderful, congratulations!" He leaned forward and pressed his lips to hers. The wine lingered on his lips, mixing with the berries to provide an alluring combination. Wanting more, she slipped her tongue between his lips, allowed them to dance for a moment before pulling away.

"I've been dying to tell someone. I tried to get Lucky alone so I could tell him yesterday but he was so busy with last minute details, and then the bachelor party. Ace and Gwen won't know until they get back from their honeymoon and I didn't want to tell my parents until things were official because I knew how they'd react." She was rambling but it felt like a weight was lifted off her chest. Finally, someone knew, and better still, they actually celebrated it with her.

"How about when we make it back home, I cook you dinner and we'll celebrate?"

"You don't have to do that." The kindness of his offer touched her.

"I want to, and don't you worry sweet cheeks, I know how to cook. What do you say? Will you join me for dinner? We'll make it back home tomorrow and I know you're itching to get back to work, so how about the next night?"

"Okay." She nodded, because dinner was the next step in seeing where what was between them could go.

"Good." He held out another berry. "I hate to be the one to press a sore subject but when are you going to tell your parents?"

"As much as I would love to hear their support, I won't get it, so I'm going to wait as long as I can. I'm sure one of my big-mouthed brothers will say something about it before I get around to it. There's no reason to fight them if I don't get it, so I'll wait, and *if* I get the contract for the space in New York, then I'll deal with them."

"I'm sorry they're not more supportive." He cupped her hand between his two larger ones. "I know it's hard because I've been there."

"Ace told me that you've lost contact with your family."

Deep sadness fogged his face. "After I joined the Navy my family moved back to Minnesota where my father is originally from. They don't care for my career and needed the distance. If I'm willing to give it up, then I can be included back in the family fold, otherwise…"

"I'm sorry." His pain cut deep within her. Her family would never disown her, at least she hoped not, over her life choices.

"As you said before, being a SEAL is who I am; I can't change, not even for my family. They chose not to accept me for who I am, and I have to live with it." He lifted her hand to his lips, gently laying a kiss on her knuckles. "I hope you won't make the same mistake they did."

"I won't." Their families' disapproval wasn't the first thing they had in common, but might very well be the strongest. "Ace mentioned before you have a younger brother, do you have any contact with him?"

"Not much. Once he turned eighteen, I thought things would change but he was in college. With our parents paying his tuition, he must obey their rules or the finances would be cut off, but even after that nothing changed." His thumb ran over her knuckles, gently caressing them. "None of that matters. The designs you need to send, do you have them done?"

"Not yet. I have some designs on my desk at home. They've been lined up for the coming seasons, but I'm not sure any of them are good enough for New York. I have a young girl, Melody, who works in the boutique. She's going to pick up a few extra hours so I can have some more time to design. Ideas are already running around in my head like demented mice, I just need to sketch them out. Once I get to work it won't be long, well, that is if I can settle on the ideas that are best for this."

"You'll find the perfect ones to blow them away," he reassured her. "I know next to nothing about the fashion world, but do you have to make the clothes yourself too? Can you do that in ten days?"

"All I have to do now is sketch them out. If they like my work, whatever ones they choose we'll design and ship to New York. I have an in-house person who does all the actual sewing. I could do it, and did when the shop first opened, but now I focus more on the designing while still keeping a hand on the other parts." She rubbed her hand along his cheek, the start of stubble pushing through his skin met her touch. "Thank you."

"For what?"

"Asking about my work. I know it's not your thing, so it means a lot to me that you let me ramble on about it." When he started to say something she ran her forefinger over his lips, only to have him suck it into his mouth. "When you're not busy with the military, what do you like to do?" The question came out breathier than she had planned, full of need, while his tongue circled the tip of her finger.

"A little of this and that. I enjoy being on the water, so I have a boat. It's not much but it allows me to get out there and do what I want. It has a small cabin, mostly a bedroom, but there's a small kitchen, so if I want to stay out on the water for days at a time, I can."

"I haven't been on the water in years. The closest I seem to get any more is the view from my condo." She tried to joke about it, but couldn't quite finish it off with a smile. "This trip is showing me more than I wanted."

He sat his glass aside, moved up next to her, and wrapped his arm around her shoulders. "Sometimes we need a little wake-up call so we don't miss the life we were given. Too bad we can't give our parents theirs, and then maybe they'd stop doubting our career choices."

"Do you ever have times when you doubt yourself? That maybe you put too much time into your career?" She shook her head before he could answer. "I guess you wouldn't. The military decides how much time you do."

"The military decides some, yes, but there's always ways for a SEAL to go above and beyond. Our team has volunteered for missions when it wasn't our turn and we do more training than others because Lieutenant Commander Mac García likes to whip us into shape when we leave off a little too much steam." He squeezed her tight against the line of his body. "You put extra time in when you love your job, there's nothing wrong with that as long as you take the time to enjoy life. One thing the military taught me is to live every day to the fullest. We're going to do that. Once the weather is nice and you've signed that big New York contract, we're going to go out on my boat for a few days, just the two of us, and celebrate."

"That sounds ideal. I can only imagine the sunsets when surrounded by nothing but water. It will be the perfect way to celebrate but I'll only go if you promise to make love to me under the stars. It's something I've always wanted to do."

"I can do that, but first I'll make love to you in front of this fireplace again, right now." He reached around her, putting his hand on her hip farthest from him, and tugged her into his lap so that she was straddling him.

"A bit of an assumption that I want you, isn't it?"

"No." He nuzzled her neck, placing little kisses along its curve. "Your body screams your desires. You want me as much as I want you."

Chapter Eight

The coldness of the cabin pulled Wynn from a deep sleep. Keeping her eyes closed, she enjoyed the sensation of being cuddled against the warmth of Jared's body, his arm still holding her tight. For the first time she realized there was nothing better than waking up next to someone you cared about. It was pure heaven, but something besides the dying fire had woken her.

She opened her eyes to find cowboy boots caked with mud and debris just off to the side of the makeshift bed. Her gaze traveled up the boots to find an older gentleman with a shotgun pointed at them.

"Jared!" The alarm in her voice woke him from his slumber.

His eyes flew open to the old man and he sat up, using his body as a barrier between her and the shotgun. "What do you want? Money? My wallet's on the end table, take whatever you want."

"I don't want your money. You're trespassing. I want you and your woman out of here." The man tipped his head toward the door.

"Our rental car broke down last night as we were traveling home from a wedding. With no cell phone reception, we needed shelter for the night. At first light I was prepared to set out and find a phone. I must have overslept," Jared explained.

"The nearest cabin is seven miles, you wouldn't have made it. That's your car on the road?" As the old man put the pieces together, he lowered the gun slightly. It was enough to allow her to breathe a little easier, knowing they weren't about to be shot.

"I'm a Navy SEAL. The distance wouldn't have been an issue," he assured the older man. "The name's Jared Taylor, but everyone calls me Boom, and this is Wynn. We apologize for intruding, but your cabin was all we could find."

"It's not mine. I watch it, since the owners only use it for hunting." He pointed the gun at the floor, no longer seeing them as threat. "I'll wait outside while you two get dressed and then I'll take you to a phone. You can call for a replacement car."

"Thank you." Her voice was mild, her heartbeat finally slowing after being scared nearly to death.

When the door shut behind him, she collapsed back onto the pillows. "Shit."

"Your mom would wash your mouth out with soap if she heard you cursing." He leaned over her, his hands sliding under his sweater, which she had put on before they had fallen asleep. "It's a good thing you got chilly, or he'd have found us both naked. At least mine would have been hidden."

"Next time I'll make sure to steal the covers then," she teased as he stood up, baring his nakedness. "Umm and what a wonderful body he'd have seen."

He grabbed his boxers and jeans from by the fireplace and started to get dressed. "Something tells me he wouldn't have enjoyed it as much as you."

"No, I don't think he would have, but I do." She held out her hands and he laid her clothes in her open grip. "I want to see a lot more of it once we're back in Virginia Beach."

"I was hoping you'd say that. Now, off with my sweater so I can clean up these blankets." She tugged her boot-cut jeans up her legs and zipped them before letting him pull his sweater over her head. His fingers ran along her sides, teasing over her hips before making their way to the sides of her breasts. "Sweet cheeks, I had planned to make love to you again this morning but maybe you'll give me a chance once we get back to your condo."

"I think we can come to some terms." The chill of the cabin had her nipples hardening, sending desire through her as if they were a direct line to her core. "I need to get dressed, it's chilly."

She gathered the rest of her clothes from where they were tossed, quickly dressing before helping him fold the blankets. Sadness clung to them, neither of them wanting their little escape to end. Now they had to get back to the real world and see if things could actually work between them or if it was just a pipe dream.

It was funny how life could change in less than twenty-four hours, and how her vow to avoid military men like the plague could suddenly seem so pointless. In a few words, Jared had a way of making her see reality, rather than what she wanted to. He was a man she wanted both in her life and in her bed.

Night had fallen long before Boom pulled the new rental car into a parking spot in front of Wynn's building. Any hope of arriving early and spending some quality time with her, maybe even enjoying a quiet dinner, some wine, and a romp in the hay were dashed when it took six hours for the rental agency to bring them a new car.

He was tired, but more importantly he was in desperate need of a shower. Food seemed overrated, but sex he'd never pass up with Wynn. He couldn't get that woman off his mind, images of her naked ran through his head twenty-four/seven like a private porno.

"I know the other members of your team were going out to celebrate last night and make it a long weekend, so I really appreciate you bringing me home." Her words pulled him from his thoughts as he shoved the gearshift into park.

"It was the best decision I've made. I didn't plan on the car malfunctioning and I know it held you back from the work you wanted to do, but spending that night at the cabin… I wouldn't change it for anything." He slipped out of the car before she could say anything and dashed to open the passenger door.

"Will you stay?"

He looked into her eyes, seeing the mix of emotions, before shaking his head. She was so easy to read, her eyes gave her away. She wanted to work but also wanted him to stay. "Tonight you'll work and rest. Then tomorrow I'll pick you up at seven for a late dinner and either I'll come back to your place or you can come to mine, but I want you in my arms again."

"Thank you. I am excited to get to work, but I'll miss you tonight."

He slipped his arm around her waist. "Me too, but tomorrow when we're both well-rested and you've had time to get some of your ideas down on paper, it will be better." With a light kiss, he grabbed her bag from the trunk.

They strolled toward the main door of her condo building, his arm around her waist. "How about I cook tomorrow? We have a quiet dinner here and dessert in bed where I can eat it off your chest."

"That sounds better than going out." The attendant opened the door and stepped back to give them room to enter. "All these years and I've never known we're practically neighbors. I'm two condo buildings down, and from my place you can see where my boat is tied."

Being back in Virginia Beach made things more serious between them. It wouldn't be long before his work started to interfere with plans, or Ace found out that his best friend was in a relationship with his sister, or one of a million other things that could interfere came up. *No, this is about us, no one else. I won't let them interfere.*

Chapter Nine

Weeks flew by with only a few uphill battles but somehow they made it through everything thrown at them. The biggest threat had been Wynn's brother, who she had done her best to deal with, though she suspected Boom was still dealing with it since he had to work with Ace on a near-daily basis. The one thing she had been worried about from the start, the SEAL duties, hadn't become an issue *yet*. Since he was home now, there were no deployments on the horizon, and training happened at their home base, she wasn't concerned with it at the moment. That could change at any moment, so she took advantage of what she could control.

Carrying cupcakes from Boom's favorite bakery in town, she strolled through the lobby of his condo building and up to the elevator. It was becoming a second home to her. If they didn't end up in her bed, they were in his. Since the wedding, they had only spent a handful of nights apart.

"Hold that elevator, sweet cheeks." She had just stepped into the elevator as he came jogging toward her in his camouflaged blue-gray Navy working uniform.

"You're supposed to be upstairs, waiting for our afternoon romp in the sack. Remember, you're the one that said you had an early day and we'd have the whole weekend. I got Melody to cover the shop so I could spend it with you." She put her hand on her hip and waited for an answer, when all she wanted to do was push him against the elevator wall and have her way with him. *Damn does he look good in uniform!*

"I got hung up with your brother. He's invited us over for dinner on Sunday, our godchild would like to see us."

"Our godchild." She held her hand out to him. "Give me your cell phone, I've got to call the papers and news stations."

"What?" He dug into his pocket and produced his phone.

"If that month-old niece of mine is talking, then we're all going to be rich and famous." She laughed at her own smart-ass comment. "I smell a set-up. How much do you want to bet Ace is determined to have one of his *chats* about this relationship and Gwen's doing it at the house so she can control how things go and try to nip my overprotective brother in the ass before he gets out of hand?"

"I could practically guarantee it." He shoved the phone back in his pocket and took a step forward to open the box she held. "Yum."

"Not until after you've changed and had lunch." She moved the box to the side before he could reach in and grab one of the cupcakes.

"I was hoping to have you for lunch." He placed his hands on her hips, gliding them up slowly.

"Maybe that's what I meant." Before she could act on her urge to have him right there, the elevator doors opened.

"Damn, if I'd have known, I'd have had you right here." With his hand in hers, he stepped out of the elevator and took her with him. "I've thought of nothing but this weekend together all week. Just me and you, in the middle of nowhere…" His words cut off when an older woman with her gray hair back in a strict bun stepped out of her condo.

"Evening, Jared."

"Mrs. Maple, I'd like you to meet Wynn Diamond. Wynn, Mrs. Maple. She's a fabulous cook, and before you stepped into my life, she always made sure I was fed."

She offered her free hand to the older woman. "It's nice to meet you, Mrs. Maple."

"Please call me Lilian." She lightly shook Wynn's hand before letting it go. "I hope you're feeding him more than just cupcakes. That boy has a nasty sweet tooth, but he needs real nourishment."

As if her words reminded him of the cupcakes, he reached for the box again, easing the lid open. She sidestepped, keeping the cupcakes just out of his grasp. "Don't worry, I'm making him lunch before he's allowed to touch these."

"Good." She nodded. "I'll see you again soon. Right now, I must be on my way to an appointment. You take care of him, you hear?"

"It was nice to meet you, and don't worry about Jared. He's in good hands."

"No doubt, child, no doubt." Mrs. Maple laughed as she continued past them.

While he opened the door to his condo, she leaned close. "You have her wrapped around your finger, don't you? Letting her bring you food when you know damn well you can cook."

"But she's a better cook than I am." He pushed the door open. "Give me ten minutes. I want to shower and change, then I'm all yours."

"I'll get lunch together. We'll eat here before we head out on the water." She tossed her overnight bag by the door before she forced herself toward the kitchen, when all she wanted to do was follow him into the bedroom.

Since he showed up in her life, she was making up for all the sex-free months. Her desires ran deeper than ever before, controlling her actions, instead of the other way around. If she wasn't working, she was thinking about him. Not all her thoughts ran sexual, but they all contained him. He was her drug; she always wanted him around. How she would handle it when he had to deploy, she wasn't sure, but she was committed. If the times they had together were always like this, then she'd find a way to make it work. Thick or thin, he was hers.

With the sandwiches made and sitting on the table, she glanced at the clock. Ten minutes had passed since the water had shut off. What was taking him so long? "Boom?" She strolled back to the bedroom, expecting to see him spread out on the bed naked and waiting for her.

"I'll make arrangements." He sat on the bed and, with a trembling hand, rubbed his eyebrows. "I'll be in touch soon." He ended the call and tossed the phone on the bed.

"Babe, what is it?" She went and knelt down in front of him, her hands on his forearms. The tight muscles under her fingers told her there was anger heating within him. "Jared, look at me."

Seconds ticked by until he finally did what she asked, yet he remained silent. "Please tell me what's wrong. If it's a deployment, we'll reschedule our weekend. Things will be fine." The words left her mouth and fear spiked within her. Their first deployment together…she knew what to expect from Ace and Lucky, but being the girlfriend instead of the sister changed things a little.

"Not a deployment." He tried to push her to the side so he could stand but she held on tight as he rose. "My fucking family."

"Whatever it is, we'll deal with it *together*," she reassured him.

"I'm not dragging you into their drama." That shook her enough for him to sidestep her and move to the window.

"Not dragging me into it? I thought we were in this together. You've dealt with my shit, put up with Ace, and now you're going to push me away?" She was no longer afraid, only angry. He was pushing her away without even telling her why.

Refusing to go to him, she rose to sit on the bed. When she looked into his eyes she could see pain, but she refused to force herself in where she wasn't wanted. She'd let him digest whatever the call was about and when he was ready he'd tell her. At least that's what she kept telling herself when all she wanted to do was scream.

Chapter Ten

The first bit of turbulence had hit their relationship in spades and Boom unconsciously tried to push her away. It didn't matter that he did it for a valid reason, it still hurt her just the same. His family was so screwed up he didn't want anyone else to have to deal with that, not if he could help it.

"Damn it." He dragged his hand over his buzz cut. "That's not what I meant."

"Then what did you mean?" She kept her tone hard, hiding her emotions.

"The call was from my mother." He clenched his fist, just thinking about the call made him angry. "My father was in a car accident…it's bad."

"I'm sorry." She shot off the bed, came to him and pressed her body against his, holding him tight.

"I've got to go to them. I'm sorry. Our weekend will have to be rescheduled." He ran his hands up her back, needing to feel her against him while he gathered the strength to deal with the curse he called family.

"Don't worry about the weekend, we'll do it later. Your family is more important."

"No, sweet cheeks, you're wrong there. You're more important." He kissed the top of her head. "They're an obligation I must deal with. It's worse than a deployment, at least then I know what I'm getting into. My family is a whole different can of worms."

"We'll get through it. I'll be right by your side."

Every muscle in his body went stiff. "No. You'll stay here."

"What?" She looked up at him, her eyes filled with uncertainties. "I thought you'd want my support."

"I do, but not there. You don't understand my family, or what you'd be getting into."

"I don't care about them. I want to be there for you. What's wrong with that?"

"You'll have to deal with their hatred toward me. I had planned for you to *never* have to deal with them." His mother's cruel tongue had already been wagging enough on the phone, degrading him. He didn't want her to have to deal with that.

"I want to be there for you." She ran her hand up his chest. "You have no idea what you're about to walk into or if your father will make it. If you're going home to a hostile environment then you need me. If you're worried things will change between us because of your family, don't be. They have nothing to do with what's between us."

"They won't curb their hostility just because you're there. It could be worse and I have no doubt that they will try to take some of it out on you. You shouldn't have to deal with that."

"I'd walk through fire for you, aggression from your family is nothing compared to that." She ran her finger over his cheek. "Where are we heading?"

"Minneapolis." Saying the name of the place his family moved to escape him sent dread through him. He didn't want to go there or see his family. Though if his father was actually dying, as his mother claimed, then it was his duty. *Fourteen years.*

"Guess that means I should make plane reservations while you pack. If we have time I need to go to my condo and grab a few other things before we leave." She rose up onto her tiptoes and pressed a kiss to his lips.

"I'm going to owe you big for this." He hugged her tight, not willing to let her go yet. "Leave the dates open, we'll fly back as soon as we know how my father is. If he'll live we'll be on a plane back tonight."

"However long you'll need," she reassured him. "Where's your laptop? I left mine at home."

"On the coffee table in the living room, my credit card is in my wallet." He nodded at the dresser, trying to get his thoughts in order.

"I'll deal with it. Are you okay?"

"Seeing my family after fourteen long years of having little to no contact with any of them makes me sick." He leaned his head back against the wall, making a solid thump as it connected. "One of the men on the team said going home always makes him feel like a child again, but for me it's sickening. They call and I jump, even after all they've said and all I know they'll do when I arrive."

65

"You go because, even though all the shit they've put you through, you still care about them. I'll apologize for saying this upfront, but everything you told me about your parents…they're assholes and don't deserve shit from you, yet I support you going because I would do the same in your case. You're better than them and this shows it." She cupped the sides of his face and their gazes met. "This right here, how you feel…it's only going to get worse when you arrive. That is why I'm going with you."

"I don't deserve you." He hugged her tight to him, lifting her slightly off the ground.

"Don't think this won't cost you," she teased. "I still want that boat trip out to the middle of the water where you're going to make love to me under the stars, just like you promised."

"When this is done I'll do that and so much more." When she started to move away to go make the reservations he pulled her back until she was pressed against him. "Wynn…I love you." He had felt it for a while now, but had kept it to himself so he wouldn't scare her away, at that moment it just felt right.

"Oh Jared." She wrapped her arms around his neck, bringing their faces as close as their height difference would allow. "I never thought I could feel like this, but I love you."

Her declaration gave him the courage he needed to face his family. It was funny, but fighting terrorists was easier than going up against his family and their disapproval. With her by his side, he'd take them and the world on single-handedly. *Watch out, here we come…*

Chapter Eleven

A cool breeze cut through the air, spraying a white powder mist of snow into the air from one of the many piles still littering the area. While the weather had just begun to turn cold in Virginia, it was already cold and occasionally snowy in Minnesota. He'd been there a handful of times as a child, but never once since his family took off running from him and his chosen career. Now this placed seemed to only hold skeletons from his past, ones he wanted to forget.

"Miss Diamond?" A man in a suit came toward them, his hand outstretched.

"That's me." She accepted his hand. "The car?"

"Right there, just as you requested." He dangled the keys in front of her. "If you should require anything else…"

"I'll let you know, thank you." She looked back at Jared, who remained silent. "If you're ready?"

"As ready as I will be." He laid his free arm at the small of her back as they made their way to the sleek black car that waited for them. "Do I even want to know how you managed to do that and avoid the rental car agencies?"

"His brother has a shop in the Mall of America, and I do custom work for it occasionally. I made a deal with him if he could have a car waiting for me outside the airport. I figured it would save time. He also has a rental apartment downtown that we'll be staying at, it will allow us to avoid a hotel and have some privacy."

"You shouldn't have had to call in favors on my behalf." He tossed their bags into the trunk.

"Don't." She leaned into him. "It was nothing and allowed us to get out of here quickly. You still have time to see your father before visiting hours are over."

"How did I get so lucky?" he whispered, his lips hovering just above hers.

"I'm the lucky one." She closed the distance, pressing their lips together, and set the keys in his hand. "You drive; you know where we're going."

"How about we go to the apartment instead?" The apartment sounded good, but what sounded better was going back into the airport and catching the first flight back to Virginia. He didn't want to be here or deal with this family shit.

"That's your choice, but we came here to see how your father is doing. If you put it off it's only going to make you more anxious than you are now."

"Okay. Let's get this over with then we'll find a quiet place to get something to eat." He opened her door for her before going around the other side of the car and getting behind the wheel. "I hope you're ready to visit hell on earth, because that's what it will be like."

"Maybe your mom will be more concerned about your father and it won't be so bad." Her voice held a tone of optimism.

"Not a chance. I've already had her spew venom at me on the phone, it will be worse in person." He wondered again why he felt any obligation to his family; after all, they never felt anything for him. It had been fourteen years since he signed the papers to join the Navy, which was the turning point in his family dynamics. Any anger he received as a child from his parents when he didn't do what they wanted him to do was nothing compared to what was unleashed the day he told them he'd joined the military.

She gently caressed his leg, pulling him back to reality. "You're doing the right thing."

"I hope so." He glanced in the side mirror until it was finally clear and he could pull out of the loading zone. The famous line, *you can never go home again* ran through his mind. In his case he wasn't going home to a house he grew up in, but home to a family that didn't want anything to do with him. Very true in his case, he had made his decision and the consequences be damned.

Wynn left her hand on Boom's leg, giving him what comfort she had to offer as she stared out the window, taking in Minnesota as he remained silent beside her. The last few hours had been tense and she just kept hoping it wouldn't be as bad as he thought it would be. Not for her sake, because she didn't care what they thought of her coming with him, but for his. Despite all his family's faults, he still cared for them even if they refused to accept his life and career.

She was there to give him the support he needed, to help in any way, and she'd do what she could to keep the family drama at bay. Hopefully then he could focus on his father, instead of flinging venom with the rest of his family. She expected his mother to be an issue, but the wildcard in all of it was his younger brother. In fourteen years they had barely spoken, so neither of them were sure how that would go. Maybe it would be the calming point of this whole mess, or maybe he'd been brainwashed by their parents' hatred and things would be worse.

Her plan was to be supportive and, not wanting to make things worse for him, she'd try to keep her mouth shut when it came to drama. With that in mind, she also knew there would only be so much she could take. She loved him and that wouldn't allow her to stand by idly while someone tore him to shreds, no matter who it was. Maybe it was the Diamond family trait coming out in her. None of them could stand by while someone was being hurt. Plus, she understood what it was like to have someone not respect your choices. Things weren't this bad for her and she never thought it would be the case, but if things were reversed she hoped he'd back her.

"I'm not very good company, but you're being awful quiet." He laid his hand over hers.

"It's fine. I was giving you time to get yourself mentally prepared."

"I'm as prepared as I'll be, plus, that's the hospital." He tipped his head forward to the large brick building as he pulled into the turn off. "Ready or not…"

She swallowed the lump that formed in her throat and nodded. "I'm ready, but I don't know about you."

He pulled into a parking spot and shut the car off. "I should have forced you to stay home but my own greed wanted you here by my side."

"I'm a grown woman and I wanted to come. You couldn't have forced me to do anything. Now let's go, you only have forty minutes until visiting hours are over." She opened her door and stepped out of the car, hoping he'd do the same because she didn't want to drag him out.

"You're worse than Ace," he bitched as he came around the car.

"It's a Diamond trait." She slipped her arm around his waist, letting her fingers travel under his shirt for skin contact. "You're here for your father. Try to ignore everything else, and let their attitudes fall where they may because they don't change who we are or what's between us."

"That's easier said than done."

"I know." They made their way across the hospital parking lot, but before they could enter the front door, she tugged on the belt loop of his jeans, bringing them to a halt. "Before we go in…I just wanted to let you know I love you."

She wasn't sure those three little words would help, but something inside her told her that he needed to hear it. It would remind him someone was in his corner, watching his back. Just as she had Ace and Lucky to help her when their parents got out of hand, she'd be there to do the same for him. They were a team. One that understood the power words held but wouldn't let that defeat them from their goals and aspirations.

Chapter Twelve

The awful stench of illness and bleach enveloped Boom as they stepped through the main doors, stealing the breath from his lungs. Hospitals were the one place he always hated. The stench never seemed to disappear, and hidden within the walls were people breathing their last. With his career death was always a possibility, one that he didn't want to think about, but being in hospitals always brought that to the forefront of his mind. How many brothers and sisters in arms did he see die over the last fourteen years? Too many.

"Thirty-one hours after the accident and you finally have the nerve to show up." Hatred slashed out like a whip.

"Aunt Cindy." He laced his fingers through Wynn's and stepped closer to his aunt, trying to keep their conversation from being overheard by everyone in the lobby. "My mother called me this morning and I boarded the first flight I could. How is he?"

"He's dying and his eldest son isn't at his bedside. How do you think he's doing?"

"I'm here now. Are Mom and Justin with him?"

"Yeah. I see you brought your tag chaser with you as well." If the look his aunt gave Wynn could have killed, she'd have been dead before he could stop it.

"Wynn is kind enough to accompany me home and I won't stand for comments like that." He glared at his aunt, unwilling to let her intimidate him. "Come along, sweetie, time is short."

With their hands still laced together, he led the way to the elevator, ignoring the people that stared after overhearing the conversation. "I'm sorry."

"If that's as bad as it will be, then this will be a piece of cake." She tried to make light of the situation as the elevator doors closed and he wrapped his arms around her.

"Oh sweet cheeks, that's just the beginning. Aunt Cindy is my father's sister, but she's not nearly as bad as my father or even my mother." The elevator crept to a stop and he laid a gentle kiss on the top of her head. "I'm sorry for what she said."

"Tag chaser? Who cares? I love you, not the uniform you wear, you know that and that's what matters."

He nodded. "I remember that uniform is what almost scared you off." The doors opened, revealing the ICU wing, and he let his hands fall away from her. "Here we go."

As they stepped off, she slid her hand back into his. "Within an hour, we'll be at the apartment downtown with a cold beer in hand."

"You make it sound like it's all worth it because there's a beer with our names on it." He tipped his head to smirk at her when he saw his mother step out of a room halfway down the hall. "Here goes nothing."

Drop him in the middle of a gunfight without any weapons and he wouldn't have been as terrified as he was now. Seeing his mother after all these years made him feel like the young kid of only eighteen who had just left home. He hated that she still had that effect on him.

"Jared." She nodded as they neared, eyeing Wynn.

"It's good to see you, Mom. How is he?"

Ignoring the question, she stared at Wynn. "You're not going to introduce us?"

"This is Wynn. Wynn, my mother Karen."

"It's nice to meet you Mrs. Taylor; however, I wish it was under better circumstances."

"I'd have preferred never to meet whatever whore he's with now." She glared at him, hatred in her eyes.

"She's my fiancée, and you'll have respect for her or we'll leave." He let her hand go and wrapped his arm around her shoulders. "I've put up with the insults when they're directed at me, but I will not allow you to berate her."

"Then you shouldn't have brought her here."

"Mom, I'll only ask you once." He stared at her, hoping that she understood that he was serious. He'd leave instead of put Wynn through the torments he had to deal with. "How is Dad?"

"It's bad. They will be taking him in for another surgery within the hour. It's dangerous to do it, but if they don't he won't make it through the night."

"What are the risks with the surgery?"

"It's a seventy-five percent chance he'll die on the table." Tears welled in his mother's eyes, the first sign of weakness he ever saw from her. "He's in and out of consciousness but if you want to see him, go ahead. I'm going to get some coffee at the end of the hall."

"I feel like all I'm doing is apologizing," he whispered once they were alone.

"Fiancée?"

"I'm sorry, it just…I hoped she'd lay off you then." He rubbed her arm. "I'll tell her the truth."

She shook her head, her hair brushing against his arm. "It will only make things worse. Let's see how he's doing."

They stepped into the room and the sickly copper scent of blood filled the air. His father lay in the middle of the bed, tubes rubbing here and there, and all he felt was regret. Regret that his father couldn't accept who he was or what he wanted to do. For most families, having a child join the military was a sense of pride, there was fear of what might happen mixed in, but never hatred. His parents didn't believe in violence unless it was coming from them. His father had a mean right hook and a worse backhand, and more times than he cared to remember was he on the receiving side of those.

He looked down at his father. The strong man had never been sick as long as Boom had known him and now he lay in the middle of the hospital bed as white as the sheet that covered him. Black and blue marks covered his face and arms, one eye was completely shut from the swelling, and his left arm was in a full cast. Seeing the injuries and knowing that most of the damage was done internally, he was surprised his father was still alive.

"I don't want you here!" His father's angry words cut through his thoughts, and he looked up to find the man glaring at him.

"Mom called."

"I don't care. Don't come crawling back now. You've made it clear over the years that the military is more important than your family."

"Damn it, Dad." He bit his tongue to keep from rehashing the same thing with his father. "I came because of the accident. We're family. This is no time for this childish hatred."

"We're not family. You deserted your family fourteen years ago." A cough racked his body until he spit blood into the spit pan. "I only have one son and Justin is on duty."

Duty? He had a brief moment to wonder what career they forced his younger brother into before his mother walked into the room.

"Get out! Take your tag-chasing whore with you. I don't want you here. You're dead to me!" his father raged.

"What's going on here, Mr. Taylor?" A woman in pale blue scrubs stepped into the room. "You know you can't get upset in your condition."

"Get him out of here!" Another coughing fit took control of his father. "He's no son of mine! I want him gone!"

"Sir…" The nurse glanced between them. He suspected she'd ask him to leave but his mother cut her off.

"I shouldn't have called you. It was against his wishes but if…" She paused and it was clear she was going to say if he died.

"It's okay, Mom. He hasn't wanted me around for years. Why should it change when he's dying?" With one last glance at his father, he turned to Wynn. "Let's go."

It sickened him to know that was it, the last tie to his family. No longer would he come somewhere that he wasn't wanted. He made the trip because, even after everything, they were family, but to be shut out and have Wynn degraded was enough for him to cut any remaining ties. People could think what they wanted, but he could only take so much, and this last bit had been enough.

Chapter Thirteen

Boom stepped into the hall, a mixture of fury and grief pouring through him. The choice he made to join the military was one he never regretted, even with all it cost him over the years: the newest being all family ties. Sure, he hadn't had much family connection since he left for boot camp, but there was still a shimmer of hope that someday things might change. Today proved that would never happen and he grieved for the lost chance.

"Wait, love." Wynn tugged him against the wall, out of the way of the nursing staff going to and from the rooms.

"What?" he snapped before he could rein in his temper. "I'm sorry." He leaned down, pressing their foreheads together.

"We've come all this way. Do you want to find a waiting room and wait to see how the surgery goes?"

"Excuse me…" The nurse from his father's room came toward them. "Mr. Taylor's condition is too grave for any type of excitement. I'm going to have to ask you to leave, if he's willing to see you, then you may try another visit tomorrow."

"We weren't planning on going back in and you won't have to worry about me upsetting him again. I won't be back. I was just hoping to catch my brother before I left."

"You don't mean Mr. Taylor's son, Doctor Taylor?"

Doctor Taylor? He tried to keep the surprise hidden, not to let the nurse know how disconnected he was from his family. "Ummm...I guess I do. Have you seen him?"

The nurse shook her head. "He's on duty in the emergency department, but he was here earlier. If you take the elevator to the first floor and instead of making a right to go back to the main entrance, take a left and at the end of the hall you'll see the sign for the ER."

"Thank you." He glanced down the hall toward his father's room. "Could you see that Mrs. Taylor doesn't forget about her own needs? Make sure she eats something at least."

"I'll do my best, but she hasn't left her husband's side except to get coffee."

He reached into his pocket and pulled out a twenty. "She won't take it from me, but on your break could you grab her a sandwich?"

"Sure." She pocketed the money and stepped away.

"Doctor?" Wynn whispered as they made their way to the elevator.

"It would seem that my father got his way. He pressed me to go to college and become a doctor, but a job like that never held any appeal to me. I don't want to be cooped up indoors, and I never could stand hospitals."

Only thirty and his brother was a doctor. He couldn't believe it. So much had changed over the years, but good or bad he needed to see where things stood between Justin and him before he returned to Virginia. "Looks like we can catch a flight home in the morning and we'll still have a little time together."

"Maybe things will change once they have time to think about it." She squeezed his hand.

"No." The elevator doors closed, giving them a moment alone as they traveled to the first floor. "Those doors have closed. It's time for me to grieve for my family and move on with our life."

"You know you'll always be a part of the Diamond family." She wrapped her arms around his waist, hugging him.

"I know, and your family is amazing, but I want you." The doors opened before she could say anything else. "Let's see about my brother and then get something to eat."

She opened her mouth as to say something but stopped as a tall lanky man neared them in a white doctor's coat. "Is that…"

"Justin?" It was more of a question to the man than to her.

"Excuse me, do I know you?

"Are you Justin Taylor?" He wanted to make sure, because after fourteen years Justin would have changed.

"Yes. Now who are you?" Justin looked between them, confusion knitting the lines of his face.

"It's me, Jared." He watched his brother carefully, trying to use his training to detect the slightest change in his brother's features.

81

"Jared." His eyes widened his mouth slack with surprise. "Holy shit, it's been too long. You heard about Dad then?"

"Too long and yeah. I was just up there, but he doesn't want to see me."

"I suspected he wouldn't. What made you come?" Justin stepped to the side to allow others to get on the elevator.

"Mom called." When Justin's gaze traveled to Wynn, he made the same introductions as before. "Justin, this is my fiancée, Wynn."

He held out his hand. "It's nice to meet you."

"You too. I just wish it was under better circumstances." She took his hand, giving it a solid shake.

"I get that Mom called, but why come home after all these years?" Justin's gaze left Wynn's and moved to size up Boom.

"Dad's dying; how could I stay away?"

"You've managed to do so up until now."

"When I first left for boot camp I used to call home, write letters, and even try to visit on leave, but every way I tried, I was rejected. They hung up whenever I called, my letters were returned to sender unopened, and they refused to allow me in when I would come back to town. How long did you really think I'd put up with that treatment before I quit trying?" Boom was disappointed that the hatred their parents felt toward him had infected his brother.

"Now that he doesn't want to see you, you'll what? Return home?" Justin shoved his hands into the pockets of his coat and glared at Boom.

"What do you want me to do? Sit around the hospital waiting for some news? Force myself into his room, even after the hospital staff asked me to leave because the patient was getting upset?"

"You shouldn't have even come."

"That's painfully clear now." Boom nodded.

"Stop this." Wynn interrupted. "You're brothers and you have your differences, but this is not the time for this."

"What do you know of it?" Justin glanced at her out of the corner of his eye, keeping his focus on Boom.

"I know enough to see that this hatred is pointless. Every child must grow up, pursue their own life, and choice of career. Jared had the will to do what he wanted no matter the cost, and it's something he has to carry with him for the rest of his life. He dropped everything to come here, even though he knew he'd most likely be rejected. That takes even more courage." She squeezed his hand before continuing. "Right now your father is upstairs dying, so how about everyone puts this hatred aside and focuses on that?"

Justin's beeper blared through the silence that settled over them. "I've got to get back to the ER."

"Dad's having surgery. Could you call and let me know how it goes?"

"What's your number?"

Wynn tugged a piece of paper and pen out of her purse before jotting the information down. "Here. This is his cell number and the address where we're staying. If you change your attitude and want to see him, you're more than welcome to come by."

"Don't count on it." Justin shoved the paper in his pocket and turned on his heels.

"What did I really expect?" Jared mumbled to himself, watching his brother walk down the hall.

"You okay?" She rubbed his arm.

"I'm fine. I didn't except anyone to be happy to see me, but there had been a glimmer of hope that Justin wasn't contaminated by the same hatred my parents had for me." He looked down at her and knew that all that he did in his life brought him to her and that was what mattered. *I wouldn't change a thing.*

Chapter Fourteen

The cool night air didn't soothe Boom's thoughts as he stood on the balcony, looking out at the lights of Minneapolis. It was stupid to come, to think he'd be welcomed, even after his mother had called. The years had proven to be a divider, one that they couldn't destroy now, one that would always be there. His only hope for the whole trip was that it might prove to be the opening he needed to gain back the friendship he had once with Justin, but even that was shattered.

"Can't sleep?" He turned to find Wynn leaning on the glass door, a blanket wrapped around her, blonde hair slightly tousled from sleep. "It's late. You need to get some rest." She came to stand next to him. "How long have you been awake?"

He glanced down, his hands itching to touch her. Awake? Heck, he'd never gone to sleep. After a quiet dinner at a restaurant around the corner, they made their way to the apartment, exhausted. He had gone to bed with her, hoping that cuddling her tight against his body would ease the tension in his body. After hours of lying there staring at the walls, he finally got up.

The smell of sweet vanilla from her shampoo and the round curves of her body hardened his shaft as soon as she settled against his body. "A bit," he lied, not wanting to explain how he'd spent the night.

"Anything I can do to ease the worries on your mind?" She slid her arm across his back, the blanket now wrapped around them both.

"There's nothing we can do here, but I don't want to leave yet."

"Melody will cover the shop, and you've got leave to deal with the family emergency. We'll stay as long as you want."

Her hand caressing his back broke the last of his control. He wrapped his arms around her, pulled her to him, and lowered his head. Their lips met, her mouth opened, letting his tongue explore. His hand slipped under the blanket, grabbing her ass to lift her off her feet. She wrapped her legs around his waist, her arms locked around his neck to draw him closer.

His groin throbbed with desire. He wanted nothing more than to take her to bed and have her scream his name. He broke the kiss, enjoying her warm breath over his face. "I should have left you here while I dealt with my fucked up family."

"Why? Ashamed of me?" Her breath came in gasps.

"Hell no! I just didn't want you to have to deal with their shit, though I have to say it was mild, guess that was because we were in public." He squeezed her tighter to him. "You know, I've wanted you since I first laid eyes on you. I don't think I've ever wanted to be with someone as much as I want you." Adrenaline flooded his veins.

"I want your hands on my body, your lips on mine. Please…" she begged.

Without further invitation, he walked the two quick strides through the door and back to the bedroom. He lowered her on the bed, the blanket discarded on the floor. Whisking her nightshirt over her head, he took in the sight of her naked body. He tossed the nightshirt aside, slid his hand over her waist, and knelt before her. He wedged his body between her legs. Trailing kisses along her neck, hunger coursed through him. He wanted to take his time, get reacquainted with every inch of her body. He claimed her nipple with his mouth, sucking it and flicking his tongue over them.

"Oh, Jared," she moaned, and tugged at his jeans.

Reluctantly, he released her nipple to lay kisses over her shoulder and up her neck until he could gaze into her hazel eyes. "You're beautiful." Her cheeks reddened as he pushed her back on the bed and crawled next to her. "I want you on top, to see your body riding mine. I want to see your beauty highlighted by the moonlight." He rolled onto his back, pulling her with him until she rested on top, caressing her curves.

He slid his hand between their bodies, his fingers teasing her and entering her, tantalizing her with yearning for more. She arched her back, giving his fingers deeper access. As the moonlight accentuated her body, she rode his fingers to orgasm.

"Please, I need you." She arched into him.

He moved his hands to her hips and lifted her. "Up." When she hovered above him, he adjusted so his shaft stood just below her entry. She slowly lowered down. Filling her inch by inch, he pushed her up with her hips before entering her completely. Steadily, his hands on her hips guided their pace.

He leaned forward, locking his mouth on her nipple and sucked until she moaned in pleasure. Her hips increased their pace, driving him forcefully into her with each pump. His thrusts became deeper and faster into a perfect rhythm. They moved together with precision, as if in a well-choreographed dance.

Her body tightened around his shaft and her nails dug into his chest. "Oh, Jared!" she cried out as his own release followed.

Breathless, he brushed her hair from her face. He wanted to see her. Wynn's eyes were glossy and dreamy—the aftermath of amazing sex. She slid off him to lie next to him and snuggle against his body. Content, he pulled the sheet over them, and he lay cradling her, caressing her spine with long, lazy strokes.

"I'm sorry things didn't go better." Her fingers rubbed small circles down his chest.

He kissed the top of her head. "Me too, but it doesn't matter."

She glanced up at him. "Don't lie to me. It does matter to you."

She was right. It did matter, but he learned a long time ago he couldn't change them. "I'm putting it behind me and starting fresh." She gave him a fresh perspective and love of life again. He wasn't going to let it slip through his fingers.

Dawn peeked over the buildings, casting a warm glow across the floor and edge of the bed from where they didn't close the curtains around balcony door. Sleep barely touched Jared through the night, and when it did, it left him with dreams of his family. Being so close to his family but so far, everything rushed to the surface. He wanted to return to Virginia, to get away from the memories that were haunting him, but he needed to stick around to see what happened with his father.

She yawned. "The time change is playing with your sleep schedule. You barely slept. Maybe we should close the curtains and stay in bed. There's nothing waiting for us anyways." She curled up in his arms, her left leg and arm draped over him, cuddling close.

"That sounds like the best plan I've heard in the last twenty-four hours. Lift up and I'll get the curtains." He slipped out of bed and padded naked toward the curtains. There was nothing waiting for them to get up, so why not stay in bed cuddled together? She had been his rock through it all and snuggling with her sounded like the perfect way to spend the day.

The doorbell rang, cutting through the stillness of the morning. "Fuck!"

"I guess that ends our quiet morning before it even starts." She sat up, grabbing the silk robe she had tossed at the edge of the bed the night before.

"Who knows we're here?"

"Besides my friend who owns the apartment? Only your brother, and my friend wouldn't stop by."

"Fuck."

"Is that going to be your word of the day?" She tied the robe. "Get dressed. I'll answer the door."

"No, you've dealt with enough of their shit." He grabbed the shorts he started the night in and cut off her access to the door. "I'll deal with him."

"*We* will, remember, we're a team."

"What would I do without you by my side?" He kissed her quickly and strolled hand-in-hand with her to the door. "Here goes nothing." Facing a terrorist behind the door would have held less stress than the idea of his brother, or any of his family being on the other side. Too bad he couldn't just shoot them and be done with it, like he could in the midst of a battle.

Chapter Fifteen

Jared tugged the door open and there stood a very disheveled Justin, his eyes red-rimmed. His stomach sank with the knowledge that there was only one thing that would bring Justin here in that condition. He stepped aside, letting his brother in.

"I programmed the coffee pot before we went to bed. It should be ready." Wynn rushed off to the kitchen.

"Have a seat, Justin." He nodded to the small living area.

"He's…" Justin started, but stopped when Wynn returned with the coffee.

"Here, drink this." She handed him a mug before going to perch on the arm of the chair next to Boom.

Justin took a sip of the coffee before setting it aside. "Dad never made it off the table and died early this morning."

The announcement did nothing for Boom. He had expected loss to set in but there was nothing. No sadness, no loss, just nothing. Years ago, he had grieved the loss of his family, so this didn't change anything. You couldn't grieve again for someone who had been out of your life for fourteen years.

"You have nothing to say?"

"What would you like me to say, Justin? Dad, Mom, and you have been out of my life for too long. I don't know the man who died today. By all means, he was a complete stranger. Do you grieve for someone who came into the emergency room? No, because you didn't know them. You do your job and try to save them, but you don't grieve for each person."

"He's your father, not a stranger."

"Justin, I really don't want to get into this with you." Wynn rubbed a small circle on his back to keep him in his chair instead of pacing the floor.

"It doesn't matter." Justin rubbed his eyes, looking back at him. "Mom wishes to respect Dad's final wishes and doesn't want you at the funeral."

"Fine. We'll be leaving soon, so there's nothing to worry about." He swallowed fury. "If that's the only reason you've come then you can leave."

"I just wanted to inform you of our father's demise." Justin stood and walked to the door. "You joined the military and that was the end of things for you, while I had to stay home and deal with our parents. You got off easy."

"You only had a year and a half until you were eighteen and then you could have done whatever you wanted." Boom didn't turn around; he didn't need to see any of the hatred on his brother's face.

"I didn't have the courage you did. All your life you went against the grain, doing things your way instead of Dad's, while I worked twice as hard to make it up to him. It's why I went into medicine. I thought it would please him, but nothing was ever good enough for Dad."

"If you don't enjoy medicine, get out of it." Boom turned in his chair to look behind him. "It's your life, and when it comes down to it, you have to make sure you're happy. You have to live with your life choices, not Mom and Dad."

"Yeah we do, and look where yours got you."

"Yes, look at where mine got me." He stood up and pulled Wynn into his embrace. "I've got a career I enjoy and I woman I love more than life itself. I couldn't have asked for a better outcome."

Justin glared at them for a moment, but there wasn't just hatred reflected in his eyes, there was also jealousy. Before Boom could comment, Justin left without another word, slamming the door behind him.

"Oh Jared, I'm sorry."

"Marry me."

She leaned away from their embrace to look at him. "What?"

"Marry me." He cupped her hand into his, bought it to his lips, and laid a kiss on her knuckle. "What I said to Justin just now is true. You are my rock. You've put up with the shit my family flung and didn't even bat an eye. I love you more than I ever thought possible, and I want to spend the rest of my life with you."

"Do you realize this is crazy?"

"Yes, but we've both always done the crazy stuff. I'm not asking that you marry me tomorrow, but I want you as my wife."

"Jared Taylor, you're all I think about from the time I wake up until I go to sleep. Even in my dreams, you play a constant part. I couldn't imagine my life without you. Yes, I'll marry you."

He kissed her, long and sensual, claiming her as his again. When their lips finally parted he whispered, "Who's going to break it to Ace?"

"That's all you." She laid her hand on his chest. "It's time for you to live up to your famous nickname and deal with the explosion also known as my brother."

"I wonder if I just got the short end of this deal," he teased.

She kissed him again. "I need to shower." She untied the robe and let it fall to the floor.

"I'll lock the door and then I'm going to join you." Watching her pad naked to the bathroom caused his shaft to harden with desire. Images of the soapy water cascading down her silky body had him quickly checking the locks before dashing after her.

In the bathroom, he could see the outline of her body in the fogged glass door. He stripped off his shorts, tossed them on the sink, and opened the door to join her. Steam billowed out of the shower. The heat of the shower called to his tense muscles, he wanted it as much as he wanted her. She leaned against the blue and white glass mosaic tiles, the showerhead spraying water down her naked body, sending soap bubbles rushing toward the drain.

"Damn, you're even more beautiful wet."

"You've already had me wet." She winked at him.

"I plan to do it again, right now." For a moment, he stood there enjoying the way the soap bubbles slid over her body. He gently tugged her arm, pulling her closer to him, and in one quick motion he pushed her gently against the shower wall. Giving in to temptation, he ran his hands up her slippery back.

He crushed his mouth to hers and slid his hand between her legs. Unerringly finding her core, he teased the bundle of nerves and dragged pleasure from her in hard, hot waves. She moaned around his unrelenting kiss. He held her captive against the wall, his fingers thrusting into her as his thumb continued to wring more pleasure from her body. "Jared." She tipped her head back, her nails clawing at shoulders as the tidal wave of orgasm smashed through her.

"Take me," she murmured against his mouth.

His teeth grazed her lower lip and he pulled his hand away. She cried out in frustration, but he ignored her demands. Gripping her hips, he lifted her and spread her thighs before he drove into her with one powerful thrust. He gave her no time to catch her breath before he began rocking in and out of her. She had no control, no say as he left her mouth and kissed a path to her neck. Digging her nails into his shoulders, she held on to him as every thrust of his hips sent pulses of pleasure exploding through her. She came apart at the seams, her inner muscles clenching around him as he continued to drive into her.

He slammed home in a frenzy and his climax burst through as a second orgasm shook her body. He held her tight until her body calmed, his hands on her hips kept her from collapsing into a heap on the shower floor. She was amazing in every way.

Wynn sat on the edge of the bed with her cell phone in her hand and tears splashing down her face when Jared came back from the pub with sandwiches for lunch. The phone call she had been waiting for had finally come in, only it seemed like the wrong time for such news.

"Sweet cheeks, what is it?" He knelt in front of her. "Did something happen?"

"New York…"

"You've finally heard from them? What did they say?" He held her hands in his, rubbing his thumb along her wrist.

"The timing is all wrong." She shook her head.

"Oh sweetie, I'm sorry." He started to get up to sit beside her.

"No, it's not that…they want my designs. It took longer than I expected for them to get back to me. I had almost given up hope, but their delay was because they wanted to offer me a larger contract. A large display and in two different Fifth Avenue shops. The contract has been sent to my office."

"Sweetie, that's wonderful! Why the tears?"

"The timing. I shouldn't be happy and celebrating when you just lost your father." She pulled her hand from his grasp and wiped the tears.

"No, this is perfect timing. I grieved a long time ago for the family I lost. Tonight we'll go celebrate and tomorrow afternoon we'll go back to Virginia. We'll even be on time for the dinner with Ace and Gwen."

"Dinner tonight sounds good, but tomorrow with Ace, maybe we should put it off."

"No way, my beautiful fiancée. We're going to take the bull by the horns and tell Ace of our pending wedding and your newest adventure to New York. Everything is going to be perfect. See, our life is coming together, one step at a time."

"You're amazing, Jared, and I love you." She wasn't sure that everything was going to be perfect but she wasn't going to fight it at the moment. Tomorrow she'd worry about Ace's reaction and what her parents would think of her branching Roll of the Diamond's designs out to New York stores, while tonight she'd celebrate with Jared and let the cards fall where they would.

 *Epilogue*

The holiday season was quickly approaching and Wynn was ready for her first holidays with the newest additions: her sister-in-law Gwen, her niece, and most of all her new husband. Christmas was only two weeks away and her parents would be arriving soon, though she tried not to think about that. Besides her parents still being opposed to her career, maybe now more than ever since she was married, all the other tumbling blocks of life were finally coming together. Finding Jared, Roll of the Diamond was doing better than it ever had, not to mention the expansion to New York being a hit; everything in her life was perfect. Even Ace had accepted her marriage and welcomed Jared into the family with open arms. They'd watch each other's backs during deployments, making sure they both made it home in one piece.

Wynn sat at the dining room table, holding her niece, Roulette. She rocked the sweet little girl in her arms, amazed at all the thick blonde hair she had. She looked more like an Angel with her blonde hair and blue eyes but Ace and Gwen had stuck with the family tradition of naming the kids after the Vegas parties the Diamond family used to host.

"I leave you alone for ten minutes and you're holding her. What happened to her napping?"

"She woke up and demanded her auntie's attention. Didn't you, sweetie?" She looked down at her dozing niece.

"Sure." Gwen set the laundry aside and plopped down on a chair across the table from Wynn.

"Where are our men?"

"I don't know, but I can tell you Ace is on baby duty tonight. I haven't slept more than three hours in the last forty-eight. That beautiful niece of yours has an ear infection and her sleep schedule is off."

She took note of the dark circles shadowing Gwen's eyes. "Jared and I could take her for the night if you want? Then you and Ace can get some sleep."

"Oh no, I'm well aware of that deadline you have with New York. I won't interrupt that with Roulette. You can have her for a long weekend after the newlywed stage, if she isn't in college by then." Gwen laughed at her own smart-ass comment. "Seriously though, I know you need to get the designs sent to New York before the holidays and with your parents arriving Saturday time is limited."

"Things will settle down after the holidays and I promise I'll take her. You and Ace need some quality couple time."

Before Gwen could comment, the front door swung open. "We're home!" Ace called.

"Shhh, my niece is sleeping." She scolded her brother, before seeing Jared come in behind Ace, looking a little green around the gills. "Hey, sweetie. Everything okay?"

"We've received word of training the next week."

Her heart sank. Training and deployments were part of military life, but since this was their first holiday season together she had hoped he would at least be able to be there through it, especially for Christmas. "Will you be home for Christmas?"

"The training should take a few days, but we'll be home for Christmas and unless we're called up for a mission we'll be home through the New Year." He laid his hand on her shoulder, giving it a gentle squeeze.

"Good." She rubbed the side of her head against the back of his hand. This would be their first actual training as a married couple where he'd be away, but since they got together she knew they'd make it through it and anything else life threw at them. They were in it through thick and thin. "It will be fine. What about the leave for New York, did you get it approved?"

Jared nodded. "Everything is set for that."

"What's this about New York?" Ace came back in from the kitchen with beers.

"The shops on Fifth Avenue that have been showcasing my work are doing a fashion show after the New Year and some of my work will be included. I need to be there and Jared will be going with me. I will also be meeting with a new shop there about another line I'm launching."

"Another line?" Gwen asked. "How are you going to manage that when you've just purchased the adjoining shop by your boutique to expand?"

"Actually, the boutique isn't expanding, the new line will take over the new shop. We're set to open at the end of January." She reached over and laid her niece back in the bassinet, before grabbing a garment from her purse and handing it to Gwen.

"What is this?" She unfolded the first dress for the line. It was a cute little Navy-inspired dress: a white top with a blue collar and a single line of America flag buttons and a waist that ruffled out into a blue skirt.

"The new line. It started when I wanted to make a few special things for Roulette. Our men inspired that one, along with a few other ones that will only be carried in the Virginia Beach boutique to cater to our military families." She waited for Gwen to look up from the outfit. "Heart of Diamond will be baby and toddler outfits."

"She got the idea when we found out we're expecting." Jared squeezed her hand.

"That's wonderful!" Gwen dashed around the table, her arms wrapping around Wynn in a tight hug. "I'm so happy for the both of you and the design is beautiful! I'm sure you'll be a success with the new branch."

She watched Ace over her sister-in-law's shoulder as he sat his beer down. "I wouldn't expect for my nieces or nephews to look anything but as if they just walked off the catwalk. You've always had an eye for fashion, not settling for the comfortable jeans and T-shirts most favor. Congratulations."

"Thank you," she whispered as her brother took Gwen's place hugging her.

"Mom's going to…"

With a wave of her hand, she cut off Ace. "Please, I know she's going to have a fit. Our parents believe that I should be a stay at home wife like Mom was, but I can't, not completely. I'll have Melody running Roll of the Diamond and I've been interviewing someone to handle Heart of Diamond, but I'm not stepping back completely. I'll focus on the designs, handle things from home as much as I can, but I won't give up or close the shops." Unable to sit while Ace towered nearby, she stood up from the chair.

"I'm not asking you to, just as I didn't ask Gwen to give up her career. I understand that you both love what you do and that's what matters. It also gives you something to occupy your time with when we're deployed. I just want you to be prepared for what Mom's going to say when she finds out."

"We'll handle your parents." Jared slipped his arm around her waist, pulling her close. "Designing and the boutiques are something she enjoys, it's time your parents start to accept that and be supportive, or keep their mouths shut."

"I couldn't have put it better myself." She leaned up kissing him. "My husband supports me, and that's what matters most. It's also nice to have the backing from Lucky, Gwen, and you. It gives me the courage to do what I love."

Filled with love, she snuggled against Jared's body. He supported her and loved her through everything, even the long hours she had been putting in recently. All those years she had refused to even consider someone in uniform had finally led her to the perfect man. The one that now had her heart. Everything was perfect. Finally, she got her very own happily ever after…

Marissa Dobson

Born and raised in the Pittsburgh, Pennsylvania area, Marissa Dobson now resides about an hour from Washington, D.C. She's a lady who likes to keep busy, and is always busy doing something. With two different college degrees, she believes you are never done learning.

Being the first daughter to an avid reader, this gave her the advantage of learning to read at a young age. Since learning to read she has always had her nose in a book. It wasn't until she was a teenager that she started writing down the stories she came up with.

Marissa is blessed with a wonderful supportive husband, Thomas. He's her other half and allows her to stay home and pursue her writing. He puts up with all her quirks and listens to her brainstorm in the middle of the night.

Her writing buddy Pup Cameron, a cocker spaniel, is always around to listen to her bounce ideas off him. He might not be able to answer, but they're helpful in their own ways.

She loves to hear from readers so send her an email at marissa@marissadobson.com or visit her online at http://www.marissadobson.com.

Other Books by Marissa Dobson

<u>Alaskan Tigers:</u>

Tiger Time

The Tiger's Heart

Tigress for Two

Night with a Tiger

Trusting a Tiger

Alaskan Tigers Box Set Volume One

Jinx's Mate

Two for Protection

Bearing Secrets

Tiger Tracks

Healing the Clan

Alaskan Tigers Box Set Volume Two

Her Black Tiger

<u>Forever Creek Shifters:</u>

Forever Fight

<u>Crimson Hollow:</u>

Romancing the Fox

Loving the Bears

A Lion's Chance

Swift Move

Stormkin:

Storm Queen

Reaper:

A Touch of Death

SEALed for You:

Ace in the Hole

Explosive Passion

Operation Family

Marine for You:

Lucky Chance

Back from Hell

A Marines Second Chance *Crossover to the SEALed for You series

Beyond Monogamy:

Theirs to Treasure

Cedar Grove Medical:

Hope's Toy Chest

Destiny's Wish

Leena's Dream

Fate:

Snowy Fate

Sarah's Fate

Mason's Fate

As Fate Would Have It

Half Moon Harbor Resort:

Learning to Live

Learning What Love Is

Her Cowboy's Heart

Half Moon Harbor Resort Volume One

Clearwater:

Winterbloom

Unexpected Forever

Losing to Win

Christmas Countdown

The Surrogate

Clearwater Romance Volume One

Small Town Doctor

Stand Alone:

SEALed Rescue

SEALed in Texas

Starting Over

Secret Valentine

Restoring Love

www.ingramcontent.com/pod-product-compliance
Lightning Source LLC
Chambersburg PA
CBHW020617130626
46552CB00003B/1013